Wounded Wind

Wounded Wind

Carlos Casares

Translated by
Rosa Rutherford

PLANET

First published
in Wales in 2004
by Planet

PO Box 44
Aberystwyth
Ceredigion SY23 3ZZ
Cymru/Wales
e-mail: planet.enquiries@planetmagazine.org.uk

Cover painting: *Hawthorn Tree* (detail) by Graham Brace
Cover designed by Glyn Rees

Printed by Gwasg Gomer,
Llandysul, Ceredigion

ISBN 0 9540881 3 1

Contents

Introduction

Galicia and Galician

In 1967, when Carlos Casares published *Vento ferido* (*Wounded Wind*), Franco's dictatorship was still in force, and life in Galicia and in all Spain was dominated by the dictator's political and cultural control and censorship. Casares was among the first modern Galician authors to produce works of biting social realism which included criticism of Franco's repression, braving the dangerous consequences these publications could have brought upon him.

Galicia is situated in the north-west corner of Spain. For two thousand years it has been known as Finisterre, land's end: geographical and political isolation throughout the ages have made it a poor region and Galician life has been marked by hardship and emigration up until recent years. The Galician language has also struggled throughout the centuries. Its time of greatest glory was in the Middle Ages, when even the kings and court poets of Castile wrote their lyric poetry in Galician. However this tradition died out from the fifteenth century and the use of Galician was relegated to the rural lower classes. It was hardly ever written, but survived through oral use.

A revival came with Romanticism: poets such as Rosalía de Castro, Manuel Curros Enríquez and Eduardo Pondal began to produce fine literature in Galician during the second half of the nineteenth century. This new interest in the language and culture of Galicia continued during the years prior to the outbreak of the Civil War in 1936, thanks mostly to the Xeración Nós, a group of nationalist intellectuals one of whose key figures was the politician, writer and artist Alfonso Daniel Rodríguez Castelao. Planet has published a translation of one of his most well-known texts, *Cousas* (*Things*, 2001). However, this rebirth of the Galician language was put to an abrupt, violent end by dictator Francisco Franco, who controlled Spain from 1939 until his death in 1975.

The Franco years were difficult ones for culture and literature all over Spain, particularly in regions such as Galicia, Catalunya and the Basque country, which have their own languages. Their use was strongly discouraged by Franco, who tried to repress all cultural and political manifestations other than those which promoted the unity and homogeneity of Spain and his own political cause on all levels.

Many Galician writers and politicians were shot, imprisoned or forced into exile. There was little literary output, but a group of authors including Carlos Casares began to write works which were politically daring as well as literary masterpieces. Yet until recently Galician continued to be widely regarded as an inferior dialect fit only for the poor and uneducated; this opinion is still held among some social groups. Since the restoration of democracy after Franco's death, however, Galician has been formally considered the official language of the Autonomous Community of Galicia, together with Spanish, and unprecedented efforts have been made for its promotion.

Carlos Casares' life and works

Casares was born in Ourense, a small city in the south of Galicia, in 1941. His father, a schoolteacher, was given a placement in the town of Xinzo de Limia, near Ourense, and Casares grew up in Xinzo and spent his summers as a boy in the neighbouring villages of Sabucedo and Beiro, where various of his relatives lived. His works, both fiction and journalistic articles, often reflect the memories of his childhood in rural Galicia during the Franco years.

From the age of eleven he studied in the Seminario Conciliar in Ourense (as a boy Casares used to say he wanted to be "an archbishop, married, with a motorbike", although he never became a priest), and this was where he first experienced the effects of political and linguistic repression. In this seminary Casares began to show his talents as a writer: he published a newspaper — in Spanish — called *El Averno* (The Underworld) which he wrote by hand and distributed among his schoolmates, and which contained fictional articles, mostly stories and poems.

When he was at high school in Ourense, in 1959, Casares won the first of the many literary awards he would receive throughout his career as a writer: a prize in a short story competition.

Some of Casares' first short stories were published in 1965 in the magazine *Grial*, which was considered a symbol of the resistance of Galician culture during the dictatorship (and of which Casares himself would be appointed editor in 1986). He read Philosophy and Modern Languages at the University of Santiago de Compostela, the capital of Galicia, and when he was in his final year his first major work was published: the collection of short stories *Vento ferido*.

The history of this book's publication provides an interesting example of the sort of tricks to which writers and publishers had to resort. Apart from being in Galician, *Wounded Wind* contains a story which is particularly critical of the régime: "Like Wolves". Surprisingly, the first edition of the work was approved by the censors (at this time, towards the end of the régime, Franco and his men were ageing and beginning to falter, and the situation was loosening up somewhat). The book sold very well, and it was decided to publish a second edition that same year. However, this time the censors decided they would not approve publication. When this unexpected announcement came, the publishing house, Galaxia, had all the books printed and ready to be distributed. With the censors about to inspect the warehouses where they were stored, the director of Galaxia, the writer and intellectual Francisco Fernández del Riego, insisted that the books must be saved, and had them loaded on to a lorry which was parked for a few days in the middle of Vigo, the city where the publishing house is based. When the censors visited Galaxia, they found nothing. Finally the books were distributed secretly among trustworthy booksellers, who kept *Vento ferido* under the counter, only to be sold when somebody asked for it. It was not republished until the 1980s.

Casares then worked as a schoolteacher for several years in various Galician towns and in Bilbao, in the Basque country.

During his years as a university student, Casares had belonged to the FELIPE (Frente de Liberación Popular de España), a radically left-wing political organisation that followed the ideas of the Cuban Revolution. Later, together with many other members of this group, he grew closer to the Partido Socialista Obrero Español (PSOE: the Spanish Socialist Party). Unlike some of his contemporaries, such as the radical nationalist writer and politician Xosé Luís Méndez Ferrín (see Planet's 1996 selection, *Them and Other Stories*), Casares did not support exclusively Galician political parties. His defence of Galician identity, language and culture was carried out from a moderate nationalist stance within the main left-wing party in Spain. In 1981 he was elected a member of the Galician Parliament. There he worked on drafting the Lei de Normalización Lingüística (the Act for the Linguistic Normalisation of Galicia) and became involved in a range of other activities related to Galician culture.

After retiring from active politics in 1985, Casares dedicated his time entirely to culture and literature, continuing his own literary and journalistic output. In 1978 he had been elected to the Real Academia Galega (the Royal Galician Academy); in 1996 he was appointed president of the Consello da Cultura Galega (the Council for Galician Culture, an autonomous institution which works for the promotion of Galician language, literature and art); and he was the director of Galaxia publishing house from 1986 until his sudden death, due to a heart attack, in 2002.

Casares, who was a keen and witty conversationalist and who was also deeply interested in Swedish culture (he was married to a Swede), wrote many novels and short stories. After *Vento ferido* he published his first novel, *Cambio en tres* (A Change of Three, 1969), which is about emigration from Galicia. 1975 saw the publication of *Xoguetes para un tempo prohibido* (Toys for a Prohibited Time), a portrait of childhood and adolescence in Franco's Spain, which was followed by the collection of short stories *Os escuros soños de Clio* (Clio's Dark Dreams, 1979); *Ilustrísima* (His Grace, 1980), a tale of intolerance narrated from the viewpoint of a progressive priest; and *Os mortos daquel verán* (Those Dead That Summer, 1987), about the Civil War. In 1996 he published *Deus sentado nun sillón azul* (God Sitting in a Blue

Armchair), which analyses how experiences such as pain, desire, love and crime change with the passing of time. His last novel, completed just before he died, was published posthumously: *O sol do verán* (Summer Sun), in which the main themes are love, death and, once again, memories of youth.

Casares also wrote children's literature, including the story *A galiña azul* (The Blue Hen), the play *As laranxas máis laranxas de tódalas laranxas* (The Most Orange of all Oranges), and a series of stories in which the main character is Toribio, a boy who loves inventing things. He was a daily commentator for Galician newspapers, and also published literary criticism and bibliographies of Galician authors.

Wounded Wind

Twelve short stories make up the collection *Wounded Wind*. They take place in Galicia in the '50s and '60s, and introduce some of the themes which will be recurrent in Casares' later work: solitude, sorrow, frustration, anguish, revenge, violence and injustice.

A number of characteristics place *Wounded Wind* within the innovative literary movement of the 1960s known as the Nova Narrativa Galega (the New Galician Narrative); they include the use of monologue and stream of consciousness, the breaking-up of the time sequence and the use of multiple narrative viewpoints. Perhaps the most striking aspect of Casares' stories, however, is their transparent, direct style which, combined with his charateristic use of understatement and restraint in expression, makes them such powerful reading.

Wounded Wind depicts the lives and experience of various characters in rural settings and small towns. The stories are told from the point of view of the protagonists, all of whom suffer from loneliness, anguish or despair. There are moments of tenderness — the boy's love for "Judas", the mother's care for her son in "Blind for Good", the childish passion of the young couple in "The Circus Girl" — but a sense of tragic fatalism overrides them all. In other stories there are none of these gentler moments at all: "The War Game", "Like Wolves" or "The Capon Cote" are grim, black texts with no glimpse of hope.

The stories transmit a forceful sense of man's impotence in the face of society and his own nature. And Casares succeeds in portraying tragic, powerful feelings by understating emotions and keeping his language to a basic, colloquial minimum. His social realism is portrayed through his linguistic realism, with its forceful concision and apparent simplicity. His sentences are in general short and to the point (except notably in "Like Wolves" and "Monologue", although in these too the language is kept simple and natural); in his minimal expression Casares reflects his characters' thoughts and speech exactly as they are, with no comfortable concessions to additional descriptions or explanations.

Wounded Wind reflects the dark side of life through feelings that are universal within a world which is, nonetheless, unmistakably Galician. The main aims of this translation were to preserve the Galician flavour of the work and its location in the Franco years, to maintain in English the style of the original — basic and direct, vivid and dramatic — and to create texts that are enjoyable to read.

I am deeply grateful to Carlos Casares for his kind assistance in many questions of detail: with his tragically early death, literature has suffered a great loss. Many thanks also to Lourdes Lorenzo for her advice and encouragement. And most of all I am grateful to my dad, John Rutherford, for his enormous help.

Rosa Rutherford

WOUNDED WIND

To my parents
To Meches and Xavier, my sister and brother
To Paco and Sira, good friends

Anyone who passes by has a face and a history.
Cesare Pavese

THE WAR GAME

They decided it by lot and I drew the short straw. I think they cheated, but I kept quiet. The Rat said: "Off you go." I didn't want to go, and that's the truth. But when the Rat said off you go, off you went. The Rat was mad, to my Mum's mind. But I think he wasn't mad, I think he was crooked and evil. "Off you go," he said again. And off I went. Don Domingo's house was far away. About two kilometres away. I had to go the long way round so as not to pass my Dad's cobbler's shop. I thought: "I'll run off home and that'll be that." But I grew afraid. And anyway it was hot and you can't stop at home in the summer for the flies.

I reached Don Domingo's villa and shouted:
"Zalo...!"
The dogs barked. I waited a bit and shouted again:
"Zalo...!"

When he showed I saw at once he'd been having a
sesta. He said: "What's up?" I said: "The Rat's waiting
at the river. He's caught a lovely butterfly. He says you
must go, he'll let you have it for your collection." Zalo
was mad about butterflies. And the Rat, what a bastard,
he knew how to tickle people's fancy all right.
"Where's the Rat?"
"In the Bomba field."
We set off running. When we arrived, the Rat was
having a swim in the river. On seeing us he got out. He
looked at Zalo with a crooked look and said: "Hullo, do
you want the butterfly?" Zalo turned towards me, ques-
tioning. The truth is, I didn't want to. The Rat whistled
and they all fell on Zalo. They stripped him and tied
him to an alder tree. Zalo was crying and I felt like crying. You don't do that to anybody and even less in such
an underhand way. The Rat spat on him here, down
here, and called him a shit-scared coward. "Boys don't
cry," he said. Then he cut a willow cane and brushed it
over his legs and his belly without hitting him. We
decided it by lot and I drew the short straw. I wanted to
run away or jump into the river, but the Rat looked at
me in that way, that way he looks at people, and I took
the cane. "Come on." I said I wouldn't. "Look Rafael,
you drew the short straw." I said no. "Look, Rafael, it'll
be you we tie up." "No." "Look, Rafael, don't make me

cross." "Look Rafael..." From his voice I could tell he was going to say that thing about my mother. I grabbed the cane and walked towards Zalo. God knows I didn't want to. And I hit him on his neck. The others shouted: "More!" I clenched my teeth and I felt my eyes filling with tears and I couldn't see. And I hit him on his legs, on his shoulders, in his face, on his chest. He was bleeding and screaming. And the others were saying: "More!" And I couldn't see. And I kept hitting. And I could feel the sun inside my head and I could hear Zalo's screams, exploding in my ears. And I kept hitting. "More!" My arm hurt from going up and down so much. "More!" When I looked at Zalo I grew scared. He was bleeding everywhere and the flies were swarming all over him. He looked as if he was dead. He wasn't speaking. The Rat and the others ran away. I ran away too.

I didn't want to, and that's the truth. I told that gentleman so, but he didn't take any notice. I also told him it had been done by lot and I'd drawn the short straw. But he wouldn't listen. He talked about hell and then I kept quiet.

Now I'm at this school. I've been here a year. It's spring and I can't get out. I might get out in July. Yesterday they took me to the punishment room? They say you can't go around on your own, you've got to play. You can't go around in twos, either. Bugger the lot of them. I want to go around on my own to think. I don't like playing football or pelota. I like playing in the bogs. And you can't. It's forbidden. But at night, when everybody's asleep, I get up and go to the bogs and play at wars. In the daytime I catch flies and keep them in a matchbox. At night I put the flies in the sink and turn on the tap, little by little, slowly. The flies crawl up, they try to escape up the sides of the sink, but I push them down with a straw and they drown. This is war. They drown little by little. It's the war game. One day they caught me and took me to the punishment room. And they called me a dirty pig for going around touching flies. So what? If it wasn't for the war, I'd die of boredom. In the winter, as there weren't any flies, I used to play with little bits of paper, but it isn't so good.

They say I'll get out in July. As for the Rat, maybe he thinks I've forgotten. He's got another think coming. Oh, Rat! He's got another think coming. I'm going to sort him out good and proper. He'll think we're friends. He's got another think coming. Oh, Rat! "Are you coming to the river?" And he'll come, he loves it. "Shall we play submarines?" And he'll play, he loves playing submarines. First I go through. I go through two or three times. Then he can go through. I open my legs and he swims between them under water. And we go on like this two or three times, for him to get more sure of himself. Little by little. Slowly. And then, gotcha, when he goes through, I close my legs and he's trapped by the neck. Little by little. Slowly. Like the flies in the sink.

LIKE WOLVES

It's all over now and the finest brolly-mender in all Galicia won't be able to sort it out and it's best to keep quiet just in case, in case they come back and give you a licking and say come with us please, as they may well say, and take you away, as they may well do, and stick you in that little room and ask where were you at two o'clock on Saturday morning? just for the sake of asking something, and you don't know what to say and they beat you into a spin and you hold out, even if you don't want to, you hold out, Eduardo, you hold out or you're done for, you hold out just like they all do, even if afterwards your friends say you haven't got what it

11

takes to be a man because if they did that to me I'd rip their guts out, oh yes everybody's really brave, aren't they just, but the fact is when they went into the bar and asked for Red, no one dared defend him even though they were all his friends, and when they said Red, come with us, please, no one objected. And now Red's rotting away and he's the one who's lost out, he died for poking his nose in where he shouldn't have, we warned him often enough, we told him often enough look, Red, you'll come to a bad end, you're on a bad road, but he was a stubborn man and took no notice, he kept on and on about all us men being equal and having rights, of course we have, we all know that, bloody hell, I know it too, but you can't speak out, you can't, you just can't and you've got to hold out and forget about your rights and your heroics, and if they piss on you, let them piss on you, for all the good it'll do them... And it's no use you going there and saying here I am, I'm Red's brother and I've come to ask what you've done with my brother, whoever it was I'll eat the wretch's liver out, because that won't do any good and they'll say they don't know, it's up to the judge and maybe they'll take you away and tomorrow you too will be found lying in a ditch. And if anyone winds you up and tells you you're not a man, you're not worthy of being Red's brother, tell him to shut up, that's life and if you're the boss you're the boss and if you aren't you aren't, I'm telling you, Eduardo, I'm telling you honest they didn't name you at all, not at all, Eduardo, not at all, my son's a witness that they said you must come with us to sort some things out, and your brother said he wasn't going, he was having a drink and he didn't have anything to sort out anywhere else and then they drew their pistols and didn't say any more and Red looked at his friends and asked isn't there a man among you? and they kept as quiet as corpses because they had no choice if they didn't all want to die there and then and at that moment Sara arrived and asked where are you taking my husband? but they didn't answer, I think they were stewed, Red was a real man and they were afraid he might fight back. They told him to get into the white van and took him off towards the Monte do Sarnadoiro. You know the rest. He was found dead with a bullet in his brain. Now it's all over. And it's best to keep quiet. The doctor kept quiet too when they took his son. That's life and that's men for you, we're like wolves towards each other, like wolves, Eduardo, I'm telling you, like wolves.

WHEN THE RAINS COME

"When the rains come, my love, what shall we do?"
They're playing it now. He shuts his eyes and sees the
couples moving silently, slowly, full of the sadness of
this slow melody that creeps in, and in, until you can
feel the tickling in your kidneys and then in the back of
your head. "When the rains come, my love, what shall
we do?"

It's been hot today. He's in shirtsleeves.

He spent the morning going from one bar to another. In
Picouto's bar somebody suggested grilling some chou-
rizos. It was Ruco's idea.

There were five of them and they were drinking.

"Tino..."

"What..."

"You've got a face like a rabbit."

"Rubbish."

"Like a smashed-up rabbit."

He's crying, now. He's no longer sure that it's because of the music. "When the rains come, my love, what shall we do?" The song has finished.

He couldn't handle his drink. He was always starting rows. Always his fault. Always giving offence. I said time and time again: "Look, Ruco, you're giving offence." But he kept on with you've got a face like a rabbit, and I said, I'm losing my patience, and he said, I don't care, and I said, you'll regret it, and he said, I'm not scared of any little wimp, and I said, don't you touch me and he kept on hitting me with his hand like that, which really hurts and sets my nerves on edge.

"Tino..."

"What..."

"I'm going to give you a shave with this penknife."

"Stop it, I'm losing my patience."

I'm going to give you a shave with this penknife, I'm telling you to stop it, I want to give you a shave, I'm telling you to stop it, I won't hurt you, I'm getting angry, you're a little wimp.

Penknives really get me. Ever since when I was a kid I had a fight with a gypsy by the river. He pulled out a penknife and poked it at me like this, as if he wanted to stick it in the small of my back.

He felt a shiver around his waist.

He gave him a push and sent him against the bar. And Ruco ran off towards the door. He stopped in the middle of the room, staggered like a drunkard for three steps, raised his hands to his chest and fell flat. His body hit the floor — thump — and he shuddered all over. Then his legs shook twice and he lay there like a rock. Little by little, on the left side of his shirt, a small button of blood was growing.

He remembers it all.

When he saw Ruco on the floor, he felt heat creeping up his throat until it filled his mouth and dried his tongue. He heard people shouting, the music, a car braking hard and hitting him on the thigh with its mudguard. For a moment he thought he wouldn't reach the police station. He leant on a man and feared he'd die right there, in the street, under that sun filling the air with a strange light. Would he some day forget the white face of that woman who'd given him a glass of cognac, in some café or other, when he felt dizzy?

A dog goes past the front of the prison. It walks along a little and then only its shadow remains, moving forward, misshapen, along the small stretch of road you can see from here.

It's three in the morning and for the third time tonight the band's playing "When the rains come..." There must be lots of people at the dance. It's hot. All you can hear is the music drifting over from the square.

A car passes by at top speed and comes to a dead stop. Even if he poked his head out between the bars he wouldn't be able to see it.

"My love, what shall we do?"

A girl's footsteps can be heard and a porch door slams shut. The car drives off.

The footsteps, the dog, the car give him goose pimples and take him far away, just for an instant, alone, to another time, far away. He doesn't know. It's like when, without knowing why, he remembers a face, a smell, the shade of a pine tree.

Tomorrow will be different.

He paces his cell.

Why does last year's festa come to mind? All the festas of old times come to mind, they'll all remain far away, empty, to be thought over lying on a bed on an afternoon of rain and tedium.

The band has stopped playing. The people's voices grow louder, they draw nearer until they're talking right here, right next to the prison. Somebody says:

"Let's go for a swim."

The reply is:

"You must be crazy."

"I bet you're not man enough to."

"Come on, keep going..."

The silence sings in his ears until he hears the whistling of a man who's about to walk past out there in front. There he is, standing still, with a pole in his hand, on tiptoes, turning out the coloured lights. He turns them out and goes away and continues whistling.

Now there's nothing to be heard.

Nothing.

A gust of wind stirs some papers in the street.

MONOLOGUE

To Paco Fernández del Riego, who is responsible for the appearance of this story here, against my will.

If she gets mad, let her get mad. What's it to me. I'll stick it out and that'll be that. She isn't going to kill me, so there. If she gets mad, fine, I'll drink, drink and sing, so there. It'll be the same old story. There'll be no shouting or screaming. I know how it goes. She won't even say I'm drunk, oh no, she knows all right. She leaves it at oh, dear God, oh, my poor little children, she knows all right. If she gets mad, let her get mad. No way am I going home at half past twelve. I'm not going, no way, so there. Teaching from eight till eight and then no fun, no, son, no way. All right, let her get mad. Oh, my poor little children, oh, oh; I'm tired.

Because a man can get tired and then, well, it's best to keep quiet because I'm getting tired of having old Chevrolet's son sitting there, in the front row, with his lardy face, because I'm getting tired and one day I'll have him down on his knees just because, because I feel like it, because I'm tired of seeing that stupid face of his, he looks like a moron, damn him, such an ass, oh, such an ass, I'm going to tell old Chevrolet to put him to work digging or stick him in a shop, the lad's no good, he stutters and can't divide decimals, lardy face, can't find words for the face on that pig. And if she gets mad, I'll get mad too, I've had enough of putting up with it, so there, it isn't bloody King Carnival's Day every day. All right, if I drink it's me who pays, I don't borrow from anyone and if I did, so much the better, if you borrow they lend at eight per cent, if your wife's expecting so what, and that's final, fifteen thousand pesetas at eight per cent and if you don't like it you can stuff it, take a running jump, they say they're doing you enough of a favour as it is, they're taking a risk, when it comes to the crunch IOUs are good for nothing, they aren't going to skin you alive, so there, and even if you end up in jail it doesn't make any difference, putting someone in jail won't give them their money back and if they send the bailiffs in that won't get them what they're owed, and if I get mad I'm going to take this glass and smash it on the floor and if I feel like it I won't leave a glass unbroken, we'll have to see how I manage in January, the fifth is on its way and although they say babies bring a loaf of good luck I'll have to pay for that loaf myself, so there. And I'm going to throw this glass at somebody's head, no one makes fun of me and I've yet to meet the mother's son who can knock me down, I'm beginning to get tired and she'll be the one, I'm getting tired and when I'm tired I'm not responsible for my actions, enough's enough, so there, peering out of the corners of their eyes at you for goodness sake, peering and peering, as if you weren't human or couldn't see them, lots of people think you're thick like old Chevrolet's son with his lardy face, someone's going to regret the day he was born. And if it's Chevrolet's son, it's him, with his ten-degree obtuse facial angle. Go on, go on, draw, you fool, draw a right angle, you don't know what it is, of course you don't know, son, of course you don't know, son, because you've got a ten-degree obtuse facial angle, oh, oh, oh, you don't know how to do it, nobody knows anything, oh, my poor little children, oh, they'll all end up backward through vitamin D or C deficiency and old Chevrolet's son and the hundred thousand sons of St Louis and the thousand greenhorns from far away, from Greenland, from the cold, who say yes, yes sir, everything's fine, everything's going fine, yes sir, and clap like this: clap, clap, clap, everybody, everybody clap, let everyone clap, you've got to clap, yes, yes, yes sir, do they think you're stupid, so there, that all you eat is lard so there, or that you have a hard time of it, a really hard time of it, because it's better looked on to say you have a soft time of it, oh, I can't stop yawning, aah... I'm sleepy, sleepish, sleepwalker, we're all sleepwalkers: me and the barman and the eighty-year-old virgins hysterical sleepwalking hopeless cases and all the hopeless people, sleepwalkers too, oh, sleepwalkers my poor little children, oh, my husband's a hopeless case, but she doesn't say it, no she doesn't say it, oh, she doesn't say it, bites her tongue, frairer shacker ding dang dong, she doesn't say it, I didn't see it, but they said it was like that: "Galicians and animals", or something like that, the sign at the station in Madriiii, piiii, I'm smashed so what, if I'm from the provinces so what, because maybe we are not human and maybe we have got an obtuse facial angle and vitamin D deficiency, certain people are going to have good reason to remember me and the Madrid chotis and now I'm off just because I want to, not because anyone's telling me to, I'll show those toffs, "Show me the way to go home, I'm tired and I want to go to bed" crowned head, Ed, dead, loaded, all to do with phonetics, ethics, esthetics, dietetics, cosmetics. I'm off. One two, three...

LONG WAIT IN THE SUN

He brushed away the flies biting his face. Then he shifted in his chair and continued staring at the white house opposite.

He could hear the noises from the street wafting up to him, monotonous, obsessive. Voices, cars, motorbikes. And the iron blows of a hammer in the garage.

It must have been about half past six. The shadow of the white house hadn't yet crept over the edge of the pavement.

In the morning his grandchildren came to wish him happy birthday. They all had lunch together. They left not ten minutes ago.

During lunch there were songs, dances. The usual sort of thing. He had to blow out the eighty candles on his cake.

"You'll get tired," they kept saying.

"Just imagine when he has to blow out a hundred..."

A hundred... It was just something they said. But their voices sounded false. Nobody expected him to reach a hundred. Not even little Ana, clean little Ana, believed what she said:

"You'll reach a hundred. You'll see."

Now he could hear the voices of the children playing under the balcony.

Every day he had a sesta. But today he hadn't wanted to go to bed. He preferred to stay on the balcony, in the sun, in the clear light of that blue sky. And to listen to the city. To listen to some music or other coming from afar.

When she was alive, they sat together and talked about the people who went past. Strangers. And they whiled away the afternoons. The long summer afternoons.

She died two years ago. She was found dead in her bed, one May morning.

The truth was he'd been sorry about her death. But he recalled those days with a certain delight: people coming in and out, shaking his hand and saying those words to him, always the same words. Several times the thought came to his mind that he'd been happy during those hours. But he didn't want to think that. It seemed a little monstrous.

He also remembered the days that followed. The

whole family would meet there, in the big piano room, to talk, to read. Granddaughter Ana, sweet Ana, played with him. She asked him things. And he answered all her questions without ever getting tired.

But then the summer came. Now they all went to the beach or out for a picnic and came back late. You couldn't stop at home for the heat. They left. He stayed behind sitting in his chair, on the balcony, waiting for the night.

He liked the sadness that came into his body when evening fell, when the first street lights appeared. He liked the fading away of the noises, of the voices, of the children's cries. And feeling the cool of the night at about half past nine, which is when they come to fetch him for supper.

The one who always comes is old Susa, the good servant who's always been with them. And she takes him along by the arm, as he leans on his stick.

Last year he could still look after himself. But at Christmas he fell down the stairs and broke his back. Since then he's been an invalid. He gets up at twelve. Luísa, his blonde daughter, comes to dress him. Then she helps him to the balcony. And there he stays until lunch time. Afterwards, he has a sesta.

He sleeps to shorten his afternoon.

The shadow's reached half way across the street now. It's seven o'clock. He hears footsteps inside the house and listens a while. It must be old Susa. For a minute he thought it might be Milo. When the footsteps stopped he called out:

"Milo!"

Nobody answered. Everything remained silent.

Milo's his oldest grandson. He's twenty and he's reading medicine. Now, during the vacations, he comes round almost every evening, to talk to Granddad. He comes at about eight and leaves at nine thirty. Today after lunch he said:

"I'll come this evening."

He waits for him to come. For him the day is no more than that hour and a half, from eight until nine-thirty, when he talks with Milo.

Milo reads the paper to him and tells him about the things he does up at the university.

The flies bother him a lot. Sometimes he puts his handkerchief over his head to keep them away. But Luísa gets angry. She says they can see him from the house opposite and that it isn't done. But there are days when these pests are unbearable. They sting like needles.

A motorbike passes by and makes a lot of noise. He sits listening to it for a good while. The glow of the welding from the garage shines in the air. And he can hear the crackles.

Some lads pass by under the balcony playing a mouth organ.

There's the sound of a door opening inside the house. It's the door of Luísa's room. Then there are footsteps in the passage and another door opening and being bolted from the inside. It's the bathroom door. Luísa must be doing her hair.

The sky's red now. Far away, looking over the roof of the bar opposite, to the right of the balcony, there's a small cloud. It's shaped like an elephant.

The bathroom door opens. Luísa's footsteps approach the balcony.

"I'm going to pick up Ramiro. We're going to the dance at the Club."

She gives him a kiss and leaves.

He remains silent for a moment, scarcely breathing, so as to hear Luísa's footsteps going downstairs. Then he hears her steps, different now, in the porch, and then in the street, different again.

Since Luísa left, each time he hears steps on the pavement, under the balcony, he wonders whether it'll be Milo. He listens for a second. They pass on. It's not him.

At the garage they slide the door shut. It's time to close up. Little by little all the shops close. For a few seconds the street remains silent. He fidgets in his chair, nervously, until a car passes by and the silence disappears.

The evening's drawing to a close. Somebody sings, a long way off, and the voice reaches the balcony. In a little while now they'll switch on the television in the bar opposite.

He waits for Milo, happily. A soft, sad piece of music would be enough to make him cry. To make him shed those small tears that don't even leave his eyes.

The telephone rings.

He can't get up. He calls out:

"Susa...!"

"Coming..."

He strains to listen. Susa's talking. She soon puts the phone down and comes over to the balcony.

"That was master Milo."

"Oh..."

"He says he can't come, he's been asked out to the cinema."

In the bar opposite they've switched on the television now. The first street lights have come on, too.

Somebody passes by underneath the balcony with a transistor radio at full volume. An old song is playing.

THE CAPON COTE

He didn't remember. Of course not. Twenty years are a long time in the life of a man. When he saw me coming into Alambrista's bar, he said: "How are you, Gonzalo?" And I played it cool: "Hullo Perucho." And he said: "You've grown into quite a lad." You could see he didn't remember. But I haven't forgotten and I don't think I shall forget even if I live to be a hundred. There are some things you just don't do. I said: "Perucho, remember my donkey?" He didn't remember. You could see he didn't. The donkey was a little one and it went around with me like a dog. I used to talk to it: "Go to the Seca field." And off it went. Once I was sitting on the flax-stone by the front door, enjoying the cool air of the evening, when Perucho turned up. "Your donkey's got into my garden and eaten some of my cabbages." And he goes straight into the stable and smashes my poor little donkey over the head with a spade. Bastard! It was at death's door for three days. It pulled through in the end, but it went mad. It was a crying shame to see it banging its head against the walls. It had to be put down. I swore to God I'd take revenge. But he didn't remember and when I reminded him he laughed like a fool. I reckon he was drunk. But I also think he realized it was no laughing matter because he was doing all he could to change the subject. He kept on asking me about Brazil, he knew those parts well, he'd been to Rio and Santos. So what. He bought me a drink. I drank. There were lots of people and I said the drinks are on me, we're going to have a party, and nobody said no and they all drank and everybody kept asking me about Brazil, on and on about Brazil and I wanted to talk about my donkey and Perucho on and on with how's Brazil these days and I said: "Do you remember my donkey?" And he said: "Stop going on about the donkey." And I said no way, no, we've got to drink to my donkey's memory, and people were getting the wind up and the barman yelling to his wife: "Dosinda, bring some more wine, it's running out!" A devil of a party got under way. To be honest, I was drunk. But even if I'd been sober I'd have done exactly the same thing. Perucho could hardly stand by now and he was laughing. "Fancy you remembering the donkey!" That was when the idea came into my head. I asked him: "You know the capon cote, Perucho?" He answered: "Yes, I do." "Let's go there for a scrap then." "All right." Off we went. He'd got old and couldn't fight any more. He could barely lift his legs. I hit him one and knocked him flat on his back. He got up and said: "Come on." I came up close. I got right up next to him. I pulled out my bradawl and stuck it into his groin, right here. Then I pulled it upwards until I felt my hands warm with blood. You could fit your fist in the hole. Over he went. Nobody said anything. At that moment I'd have ripped anyone open. People don't get cocky with me.

BLIND FOR GOOD

I asked Mother: "Will I be blind for good?" She answered: "No." But I don't believe it. This morning, when they took me to the yard balcony, feeling the sun had settled on my skin, I said: "Let's see." I poked this finger in at the corner of one eye, lifting the bandage up to see if I could see anything, but I couldn't. Not even a tiny glimmer. Nothing. I'd half come to terms with the idea already, because on Santa Lucía's Day Mother took me to Paredes for a cure. Though they tried to fool me, it was clear to see that the pilgrimage was for me, because they didn't let me have any fun. But my sister played all along the way, picking foxgloves and chatting with people. And me all quiet and Mother saying: "Say a prayer to Santa Lucía." And me praying against my will because the sun was hot and the way was long and rough, about two leagues of it all across the hills. I remembered when they took my sister to San Benito and they didn't stop pestering her either, making her pray like me now. She wanted to play with me, but they didn't let her. And yet I did as I liked and nobody told me off. And it's easy to see that nowadays I do what I like at home and Mother doesn't ever get cross with me and it's always: "Would you like a little honey, pet?" "Would you like some sugared wine?" "I'm going to bring you white bread back from town." It's plain to see it's because I'm blind for good. Yesterday they told me off for saying I didn't like Camilo any more for hitting me with the stone, but they only told me off yesterday. And whenever Mother mentions Camilo she says he's a good boy and he didn't do it on purpose, it can happen to anyone. Mother says that because she knows I'm blind for good and so that I won't hold a grudge against Camilo all my life. From now on I'll be like Nicolás, who taps his way from his house to the threshing-floor or from his house to church. And that's as far as he goes. And you can see Father's sad because he hardly speaks and the day before yesterday, when I fell asleep at lunchtime, he woke me up and said: "Did you sleep last night?" I answered I had, but it wasn't true. For more than a week now I haven't slept a wink. When I get into bed a black sadness creeps into my heart and my blood gets all full of little ants and I hide deep down and cover my head and pray. But praying doesn't make it go away. And I carry on praying so as to go to sleep, but I must be very bad, I've already come to terms with my blindness being a punishment for my sins. She doesn't now, but before Mother did keep saying: "You're a sinner and you'll go to hell." And it's plain to see I shall, because I pray and God takes no notice and I can't sleep... Next summer I've got to go back to Santa Lucía for a cure and I won't feel like playing or popping foxgloves. And if the sun is hot, I'll just put up with it, because that way I'll do penance for my sins, too. Just now the sun is hot. I poke my finger in here, at the corner, and I can't see anything. Mother calls to me: "Ramonciño." "Yes, mother." "Are you all right?" "Yes, I'm all right." "Do you need anything, my pet?" The sun must have gone down behind Mount Picouto. You can't feel its heat any more. In a little while it'll get dark. Then we'll have supper and afterwards we'll all go to bed. Just thinking about it makes my blood fill with ants and a great, black black sadness creeps into my heart.

THE THUNDERSTORM

He went to the door and looked up at the sky. It was blue. Someone asked from inside:

"What's the weather like?"

"No clouds in sight yet," he answered.

But he was sure. It had to come. His leg ached and he felt as if there was a wasps' nest in his heart.

"You'll be proved wrong."

He went back inside and thought: "I won't be proved wrong, I won't." He sat down on a bench and asked for another drink. The flies were making a noise like people praying. He remembered a thunderstorm in the year 1940. The harvest hadn't even been enough for the next sowing. It had come at about this time of year, too. And it had come in the same way: an ache in his left leg and not a trace of a cloud. The sky was blue like today. Then, great black clouds had begun to gather over the Pico do Mediodía until the beginning of that continuous low rumble which carried on well into the night. It had taken everything away.

The barman says:

"There'll be hail and all."

"There will."

"Better if there weren't."

He didn't feel like talking. Now his head was hurting too. In two or three hours, he knew, the back of his neck would be aching. Then he would have no choice but to throw himself down under the lean-to, on the grass, writhing like a sick dog. And be like that all night long, without a moment's sleep, to get up the next morning with swollen eyelids and a numb forehead.

At half past two they rang the bells. And before long the first claps of thunder were heard, far away. People started to appear at the bar. They were gathering together. They were looking out of the window, towards the street, which was gradually filling with an ashen light. The earth smelled of burning. Nobody spoke.

A flash of lightning lit up those fearful faces. Then the walls trembled.

"There it is."

The women shut themselves up in the back room and burnt bay leaves.

It hailed all afternoon. The hail broke tiles and window panes. It killed birds.

When it had cleared, they went out.

He was left alone. His temples were bursting. He spat and thought: "It's done away with everything." This year the ears of corn were full. They bent over under the weight. He said to himself: "This'll be a year of hunger." Only the broken straw would be left, lying over the irrigation canals, all tangled up...

In the street he came across the people who were returning from the cornfields.

"All gone."

He took himself upstairs. He was tired. He pressed his forehead against the window in his room and that relieved him a little. He loaded his shotgun and went down. He took the donkey and went towards the Fontemoura field. He was burning inside. His heart was jumping in his mouth.

The sky was still black. Lightning still flashed behind the Pena Alba. A soft, sad wind rustled the leaves. It was the only sound. Everything else was still, silent.

They found him with his face smashed like a squashed tomato.

And beside him lay the donkey, with a trickle of blood leaking from its mouth.

JUDAS

They called him Judas. He didn't know why. He went around begging. He entered the bars at night and they'd say: "Judas, dance a rumba." He'd dance. "Judas, sing." And he'd sing "Granada". He always sang "Granada". When he finished he passed his cap round and they threw in a few coins. He also knew two stories: the one about the priest and the hen and the one about the dim-witted boy. He charged one peseta for telling the story about the priest. And he charged five for the one about the dim-witted boy.

The stories had been taught him by old Tomás, a cobbler who lived on the river bank and had a boat.

He'd also taught him how to use birdlime. Old Tomás knew lots of things. Some said that he was a witch, that he drank blood and told fortunes. But it wasn't true. People didn't like Tomás, because he was a republican. One day they took him to prison for saying "Long live equality!" to a civil guard who tried to beat him up.

Old Tomás was ill. People said he was going to die.

Judas thought this could be true, because the old man wasn't what he used to be. He never spoke and didn't mend shoes any more. He just got into his boat every now and then for a trip down the river and was tired when he came back. "He won't last long," he thought.

"Is anything the matter, Tomás?" asked Judas.

"No, lad."

But old Tomás wasn't the same. He whiled away the hours sitting at his front door, pondering.

"What are you thinking about, Tomás?"

"I'm thinking about life."

From then on, when Judas saw him like that, silent, he didn't say anything. He sat down beside him and kept still so that old Tomás could think about life.

He went every day to see him.

"Here are ten pesetas I made yesterday."

"No lad, I don't need any money."

On the third day he took them and thanked him. After that he always took them. And thanked him.

One morning, old Tomás couldn't get up. He couldn't stand. He was white and you could barely see his eyes. At about two he called Judas and said:

"I'm going to die, lad."

And he didn't speak again. At seven he died.
They buried him the day before yesterday.

The downpour came all of a sudden and people ran for shelter under the colonnade. Lightning flashed. A blind man, alone in the middle of the square, walked along slowly, soaking wet already, trying to find shelter. A bootblack was listening to the sports news on a transistor radio. You couldn't hear it clearly for the storm. There was a strange smell in the air and it was hot.

The lad looked at the rain, pouring down on the parked cars.

It kept raining all afternoon. A young couple complained that it was a bore.

As it didn't stop raining, the lad set off running. He went into a bar. It was full. They called from the end of the room for him to go and sing. He sang "Granada". They bought him a drink and even gave him a bit of octopus. He danced the rumba. And he told the story about the priest and the hen and the one about the dimwitted boy. He drank some more. He drank and sang until the people began to go round and round in his head. He shouted "Long live Real Madrid" three times running, he called a lady a whore and they threw him out. Off he went. A wet dog was walking along as if it didn't have a master. He called out to it: "Good boy, come here, come here, boy." The dog went up to him, smelt him and ran off. Judas laughed and said: "I am a dog." A woman was walking past and Judas asked her for a peseta. The woman gave it to him. The lad looked at her and barked: "Guau, guau!"

At two in the morning he took the barracks road. He stopped in a small square lined with houses that had broken windows. No sounds reached this place. He went into a porch. He lay down on the first landing. His head ached. The cathedral clock struck three. Then everything was quiet. He spent some time trying to find a good sleeping position. Suddenly a strange fear came into his body. He felt goose pimples. His mouth went dry. He ran down the stairs three at a time.

The small square was deserted.

He needed to vomit and went and stood by a wall. He vomited.

It was thundering. He wanted to have a pee. He looked up at the sky. He said: "I am a dog."

The wind began to blow.

The summer was coming to its end.

THE CIRCUS GIRL

He looked out of the window. The big top could be seen high among the oak trees in the fairground.

He's been punished. When he gets out, the afternoon session will have finished. And after supper they won't let him go.

It all started because of a bet. The fifth years' classroom was class II, and you went to it directly from the entrance without passing through the other parts of the school. They could see the street and tease the girls walking past without anyone watching over them. When they saw Anne, they called to him:

"Here comes the little French girl from the circus."

He'd met her by chance. One afternoon, at around six, he was sitting on a bench in the park and noticed that coming towards him was a girl with long blond hair, wearing shorts. She asked him in a French accent where she could find a doctor. He went with her. On the way she told him that she was a trapeze artist at the circus and that her father, who had been a gendarme, was ill (nothing much: indigestion perhaps), and that he'd asked for a doctor. He hardly spoke. When they reached the clinic he told her: "Here." She thanked him and said he could go to the ticket office, where she'd leave him a couple of tickets for the eight o'clock show.

He went. Before climbing up to the trapeze, the girl, dressed as a fisherwoman, sang a song. Halfway through it she turned to the seat where he was sitting and cast the fishing-line towards him, while she said, as everyone laughed: "Bite, bite, little fish."

They met again the next day.

After that they saw each other every day. They spent the afternoons down by the river. They lay down on the sand. They buried themselves. They swam. She spoke to him of Marseilles, of her childhood. He closed his eyes and imagined that street opposite the port, the ships that Anne waved goodbye to with a white handkerchief from the loft, Aunt Françoise, Jules... What was he like, that Jules, who had given her her first kiss in the porch?

"He was blond like me. With lots of freckles."

"Do you think about him?"

He had a straw hat over his eyes to keep out the sun. Again he asked:

"Do you think about him?"

He felt her lips settling on his. It was like a whiplash. A white joy was being born inside his heart.

Then they kissed. They kissed many times. And she rested her head on his chest.

Soon the news spread that they were seeing each other down by the river. His parents told him off. "That was all I needed," his father had said, "a circus artist for a son!"

But they carried on seeing each other in secret.

Today his fifth-year classmates challenged him.

"Bet you're not man enough to make her come up here..."

He didn't hesitate. He leant out of the window and called:

"Anne...!"

She came up. He met her in the entrance hall and they went into the lab. They locked the door and blocked up the keyhole with a piece of paper. The fifth years were making a din outside. He showed her the butterflies, the stones, the lizards and the snakes in formalin... He asked her for a needle and pricked his finger. He showed her the blood under the microscope.

"You know what?" she said.

"What?"

"We're leaving tomorrow."

He caught her around the waist and kissed her.

And at that moment the headmaster arrived.

By the time he gets out, it'll be dark and he'll have to go home without seeing her, without explaining, without telling her what happened. And after supper he'll say: "I'd like to go to the circus." And his father will answer: "No." Then he'll go to bed. And he'll think: "Old people don't understand." And the old people (not so old) in their bedroom won't even remember him and the little French girl Anne. And he'll take a long time getting to sleep, but he'll sleep. Will he?

Tomorrow, when he gets up, he'll feel sad. Sadder than anyone. And what will become of Anne? He won't see her again. Never again? Never.

He got up very early. He ran off to the fairground. All that was left where the big top had been was a circle.

THE OTHER SUMMER

The dance goes on.

As she sits on a stone bench in the Alameda park, on her own, she doesn't see anybody.

She arrived early this morning. Her aunt and uncle were waiting at the station. She spent the day checking out the old familiar things: the piano key that clunked and set her teeth on edge. That newspaper from the year 1912 that someone had put away, God knows when, at page 12 of the Raimundo de Miguel Latin dictionary. The dust on her work table. The key to the great front door that was still hanging behind the library door, as always. She played with Pin, the little dog she had named three, four, five years ago... how long was it? She walked in the garden and drank, she wasn't thirsty but she drank, from the Carpazal fountain. It was in the garden she realized this summer would be different. Standing on top of the garden table she looked far across the countryside to the quarry of the echoes. It was Sunday and the quarriers weren't at work. She tried to remember: "We children climbed to the top of the Penamoura and the grown-ups stayed...," but she thought: "No." And she went back to the house. She couldn't quite remember, but somewhere she'd read that, sometimes, the Sunday air was different. She said: "Today it is, too." She heard her own voice in the solitude of the room and listened a while. She was sad.

 After lunch she lay down on her bed for a rest. Once again she counted the thirty planks in the ceiling. Then she closed the windows and amused herself watching the shadows of the people passing by on the street, reflected, like skeletons, on the white wall at the far end of the room.

She slept.

When she woke it was supper time. During supper her aunt and uncle talked a lot. They'd go on various boat trips, on the ria, and if she extended her holidays a bit they could go to Portugal at the beginning of October. She said she wouldn't be able to, but they answered that they'd talk about it again later. What's more, as they were getting on and didn't know how to have fun any longer, it wouldn't be a bad idea for her to go out with some friend or other. That way she'd have a better time.

She's gone to the dance. She sat down on a stone bench and there she is, pensive, her hair falling over her eyes, sad, a little tired. From time to time she looks up at the people dancing, she looks with great care, but then she draws inside herself again, deep inside, forgetting everything, absent almost.

The couples dance, rotate, move slowly, bewitched by the rhythm of the band playing, playing on and on, the master of the atmosphere, the master of the bodies by now. And she looks, she looks among all the people once more. Before long she'll realize that she isn't going to find anything there, but she still has a flicker of hope.

She isn't bored. She picks up a stick and draws a circle on the ground and a triangle inside it and two crosses. Then she rubs it all out and writes "Mónica" and rubs it out again and stares at the sand under her feet and strains her ears as if trying to escape from the music to get to the beach, to the noise of the waves breaking on the rocks, breaking, which she hears breaking now, breaking into her head just like when she listens to sea shells. And then her thoughts cloud over, among tears that she doesn't weep, but that hit against her eyes, her thoughts cloud over and now she doesn't know that she's at the dance in the Alameda park and that she's waiting for something, almost unwillingly, but she's waiting, she'll wait a little longer, just a little, before that flicker of hope inside her dies away for ever. She forgets everything and the sea calls to her in her memory, it calls to her powerfully, imperiously, while she tosses her hair back in an absent, mechanical fashion, because on the beach a boy says you're looking very pretty and she feels as if sand was pouring into her and the boy takes her hand and they kiss and swim together and the sun tans them, intoxicates them, and she says nothing because the boy talks, and talks, and talks and she doesn't want to think about anything or hear anything, she just wants to dream, dream, she just wants to dream and spend the afternoons on the island dancing with their feet in the water and their faces close, holding each other, electrified climbing that hill of fire, climbing among the embers, climbing until that powerful force splits into little coloured lights and nothing's left but hot smoking memories, running to see an Italian film that she'll see again later in the rainy winter city, telling her friend all about it, crying, not out of rage, nor disillusion, but out of sadness or boredom, crying first without really knowing why, then because of the rain, because there's no sun, because there's no sea, because she has no beach, because she has no him, crying and answering one letter after another after another until one day she stops writing because she doesn't feel like it and her memories don't mean much to her any more in the cocktail bar, chatting with other lads, dancing, saying what sign of the zodiac are you and I like twenty-five-year-old lads and he was a kid of seventeen, what an idiot, how time passes, what an idiot one is on occasions. And it doesn't stop raining, it rains on and on, and Sundays begin to be nasty and people fill up the cafeterias and the bars, and they talk loudly and she dances, she dances and she can be happy, and on Santa Cruz Day she caught herself speaking to her mother about something they had never spoken about, cousin Carme is expecting and she blushes and the springtime sun returns, the sun, the sun that begins to caress those white legs, tanning them and she puts away her tights till another winter comes and her father says you'll go on your own to spend summer with your aunt and uncle.

The band has changed rhythm now.
She can't hear the sea any more. A lad goes up to her and says:
   "Will you dance?"
   She looks at him and without saying anything she gets up and they dance.
   The lad asks:
   "You aren't from here, are you?"
   "No."
   She doesn't feel like talking.
   "What's your name?"
   "Mónica."
   "Mónica? Like Mónica Vitti."
   But she doesn't answer, she doesn't say anything, she's sad and thinks she's a fool because she has all summer before her with the beach, the sun and the sea. The music rotates and she rotates and the couples rotate. With each turn, she looks among the people, she looks for the last time, because now she knows that however long she waits, he won't come.

SHE'LL COME ROUND THE CORNER

At this moment he raises his eyes from the magazine and looks out of his compartment window. What only a while ago was just a glow is now light, certainty.

The travellers begin to wake up, languidly, in silence. The person sharing his seat, a fat lady, asks:

"Is this Ávila?"

He doesn't know, but he says:

"I don't think so."

Then he gets up and goes to the toilet. He catches sight of himself in the mirror. He is pale and has rings under his eyes. He hasn't slept all night long. He thinks: "Stands to reason." He plugs his electric razor in and has a shave. The sound makes him start to nod off. He slaps himself on the forehead. He washes his face and goes out into the corridor.

The sun comes in through the window and makes his eyes ache. He feels sleepy. He holds on to the metal bar and rests his head. The clickety-clack of the train sets him a little apart from reality. Someone by his side says:

"In Madrid the month of August is terrible."

He doesn't care. He's unsure whether he finds it easier to put up with the cold or the heat. But he doesn't care.

He woke up at the station. He was slightly nervous. He hailed a taxi:

"Bárbara de Braganza Street, please."

Once inside the taxi he stretches his legs and tenses all his muscles, but his nerves still prickle on his body as if someone was tickling him around the waist and on the chest. It's an old feeling. How many times has he repeated the same movement, inside a taxi, on the way to this same street? When he gets out it'll be worse. And the most disagreeable moment, when he rings the bell. After that, calm and deep happiness will come.

Now he's in front of the house. From the pavement he looks up at the second floor. He goes into the porch and climbs the stairs. He climbs them slowly. A man coming down greets him: "Good morning" and he uses the excuse to have a rest, but he leaps up the last few steps three at a time. He rings the bell. He listens a while and hears muffled footsteps coming from the far end of the flat. His heart is jumping in his throat. He smiles. The door opens. In front of him stands a girl in a white apron.

"Miss Clara?"

She answers she's not at home, she went up to the serra with some friends, they must have left about two or three hours ago and by ten this evening she should be back. No, she doesn't know where they might have gone. She didn't say.

That's all he wants to know and he leaves. He doesn't hear the voice of the girl in the white apron asking if he'd like to talk to Clara's parents, because he's far away, going over letters in his memory, remembering certain sentences that perhaps mean there was already a sign of something. But he can't remember properly, he can't remember anything because the whole of his head is on fire and objects, houses, cars, people are dancing in his eyes.

He has spent all morning wandering round the streets, going nowhere in particular, feeling a slight oppression in his chest, until his legs started to be heavy as if they'd been filled with stones. He went into a bar and after lunch he felt better. He sat down outside a café for a coffee.

He looks at his watch two or three times. Finally he puts it forward twenty minutes. He knows he's kidding himself, but he puts it forward.

Opposite him he sees a big cinema billboard. He stares at the figures: a couple kissing. Each lad that passes by is hatred spreading in his heart. The entire city is, by now, a hot darkness inside him. He turns his chair around because he doesn't want to see people and sits facing the road, with cars going up and down that will make him feel, that are making him feel somewhat dizzy. Then he shuts his eyes. And she suddenly springs up in his memory:

"I look forward to these days all year long."
"Do you really, Clara?"
"I spend all my time looking forward to them."

But that was long ago. Then came a few letters and a sentence: "I'm tired" and then later on: "I have my doubts." He got angry and stopped writing for a month.

Now he's here, sitting in a bar, waiting for his watch to say it's ten o'clock.

He gets up and leaves.

He goes into a cinema. That way time will go by quicker.

When he goes out it's twenty to ten. He takes a taxi and says mechanically: "Bárbara de Braganza Street, please." And the taxi drives off. The flashing signs are a pulsation of colours in the street.

He sits down outside a bar on the pavement opposite. There are lights in Clara's house. He drinks a glass of cognac. His heart is thumping inside him. He fidgets in his seat. Again he feels tickles around his waist. Before long she'll come. She'll appear at the bottom of the road, coming round the corner of Castellana Avenue, holding a lad's hand. And he'll sit there — he thinks — without doing anything, without even calling out to her, without saying: "Hullo, Clara." Nothing. And afterwards — he carries on thinking — he'll get up and go inside the bar. He'll pick up the telephone and say: "Clara, I'm out here opposite your house." And as for her, what will she answer? He doesn't care. He knows that tomorrow he'll go back to his town and that this winter the classes at the University will be more boring than ever and on Sundays it'll rain and he'll go to the café with his friends to crack jokes, to talk about the girls walking past the front window. And he won't even be left with the faint hope that summer will come.